Gerhard Roth

The Will
To Sickness

translated from the German
by Tristram Wolff

Burning Deck, Providence

DICHTEN = is a (not quite) annual of current German language writing in English translation. Most issues are given to the work of a single author.
Editor: Rosmarie Waldrop.

Individual copies: $14
Subscription for 2 issues: $25 postpaid

Distributors:
Small Press Distribution, 1341 Seventh St., Berkeley, CA 94710
1-800/869-7553; www.spdbooks.org
Spectacular Diseases, c/o Paul Green, 83b London Rd., Peterborough, Cambs. PE2 9BS
H-Press, www.h-press.no

for US subscriptions only:
Burning Deck, 71 Elmgrove Ave., Providence RI 02906

Burning Deck is the literature program of Anyart: Contemporary Arts Center, a tax-exempt (501c3), non-profit corporation.

Cover by Tristram Wolff.

ISSN 1077-4203
ISBN 1-886224-78-1

Contents

I. The Story So Far

EVERYONE THINKS I should be motivated, so here in my darkroom I develop carefully gauged phrases and body language that make me appear so, thought Kalb. He turned on the faucet and the stream ran over his palm, transparent.

KALB woke one morning to a sky so soaked with air it had turned a deep blue. Someone knocked. Kalb did not stir from his burrow in amongst the bedcovers. Wessely took a seat on the chair. Shutting the window Kalb caught sight of himself for a moment in the mirror of the windowpane: his eyeballs looked exactly like a set of fried eggs.

I N THE CAFÉ he was greeted by Dr. Slama. He was wearing new gloves. He showed off how black-berry-black they were, quite pleased with himself. The frame of the mirror mounted on the wall was gilded as ever and had already begun to come off in flakes. Here was the waitress. She was dressed all in black except for her little cap. Wessely on the other hand wore a yellow shirt that showed up again in the marble tabletop. Kalb's color-sensitive cones were behaving very well; they dealt effortlessly with the shifting wavelengths of the light. Kalb anticipated what would come next: for instance, whether a person carrying a blue porcelain object would come by, or a person with shoes the color of sand might take a seat at one of the tables, maybe with a blood-red tie cleaving his torso like a gaping chest wound. Whereupon Dr. Slama gulped down an entire serving of vanilla ice cream. This pleased Kalb more than he — or indeed anyone else — could know.

KALB examined his thumb under the lens. The thumb sat upon a housefly. He applied pressure. As the fly's legs flattened away from each other drops of liquid oozed from its body. Kalb rubbed the fly's remains off the end of his thumb. He wiped them off on the window. Thinking better of this, he scraped the fly from the glass, threw open the window and flicked the thing out into the air.

BEFORE KALB, the electric stove — the water was boiling in the enamel pot —, the saltshaker, the tomatoes, the kitchen knife. Kalb stood up. He walked over to the mirror. After inspecting his hair for some time, he ascertained that his scalp was dry and scaly. Kalb's cat sat under the washstand. He undressed. Musingly he smoked a cigarette. The cat sat under the washstand and stared at his crotch. As he pulled the plug on the dirty water, the drain was suddenly stopped up with hair. Kalb dried the hair on his head. The cat sat now crouched on the sideboard. Kalb hung the hand-towel back up on its nail. He brushed his teeth. He spat out the toothpaste, with some blood from his gums, into the sink. After shaving he scrubbed his face with eau-de-Cologne. He cut himself shaving as always and bled a few drops. In the greater scheme of things it was all the same to him. He took a pair of nail-scissors and trimmed his corns. He slipped on some clothing. He gave the cat the callused skin he had clipped from his corns to munch on. The cat went at it gamely. Kalb put the flowerpot with the geraniums in full bloom on the table and ate up the tomatoes, since it was already ten o'clock and he had not yet breakfasted.

S OMETIMES KALB had to wonder at how beautiful a
splintered wash basin appeared to him or a bathtub
or a bathroom painted over with oils or cracked tiles or
dirty towels or used soap bars.

H E STOPPED short. A storefront was stuffed with prosthetic arms and legs. The prosthetic limbs were modeled on reality and very life-like, even the joints looked functional. Kalb inserted the image into the projector and screened it in his brain.

A LITTLE LATER he entered the apartment building. A door opened and a girl stepped out, her face covered in purple eczema. Before Kalb could say a word, the girl had disappeared into one of the adjacent apartments, abandoning the enchanted Kalb like an apparition.

THE SYMPTOMS of sickness, wrote Kalb, must be considered as works of art. Think of the spectacle of a blind man tapping along the sidewalk with a cane, or a one-legged man with crutches — or imagine the beauty of epileptic fits, when the body thrashes around on the floor, or the aesthetic effect of a hemorrhage spreading over a sheet! So many images flashed through his head in that fraction of a second: skin-ulcers, jaundice, imbeciles, cretins, hydrocephalitics, smoker's legs, abscesses, sclerotics, dropsy patients, etc.

II. Report from Kalb's Life

S INCE EARLY THAT morning, some alien bit of matter in Kalb's eye had caused an irritation of the cornea, or rather of the bulbar conjunctiva. Kalb had tried to dislodge whatever it was by fluttering his eyelids open and closed, but the feeling of discomfort lingered. So he went to the mirror, and pulling the lower lid sharply downward with one finger, took hold of the upper lid by the eyelashes and pulled it cautiously down too. He felt around nervously for the toothpick he'd laid ready. Using the toothpick he folded his eyelid up and back over itself so that the under-lid was totally exposed. He took up his handkerchief again and dabbed at the eyelid's lining. A bit later the alien matter seemed to have gone. Kalb noticed a speck of soot on the corner of his handkerchief.

H E SAT DOWN in the streetcar. It was only now that one particular stranger's outfit caught his eye. Despite the relative heat the man had on (among other things) a duster which, at that very moment, he pulled more tightly around him with a shiver, as though freezing. In the course of the ride Kalb perceived a streak of blood on the stranger's left shirt collar, evidently the result of a shaving mishap. His gaze lost its hold and crashed to the floor. The stranger turned toward him sharply. Something he could do for Kalb? Kalb answered: No. He forced himself to look out the window. The window glass had been smashed in and patched with cardboard. Through its cracks streamed the copper-green color of the dissolving vault of air.

B USILY his brain produced ideas and laid them out
for inspection.

KALB, like all other living creatures, was nothing more than a chemical machine. This machine's precise steering system and high efficiency was effected through a certain class of proteins, enzymes that acted as specific catalysts. Also like a machine, the organism "Kalb" represented a coherent and integrated functional unit. The stability of the functional coherence of such a complex and, moreover, autonomous machine made a cybernetic system essential, which continually guided and controlled its chemical reactions. So much for the organism "Kalb."

A GUST OF WIND turned the umbrella inside out. Kalb pushed against the IN door. Behind the door stood Wessely. Kalb's underpants were like damp towels. Wessely laughed. The rain let up a little. Kalb shook the raindrops from his jacket and went back out into the street.

HE SOAKED UP the things surrounding him until his skull was full. He sucked and sucked, but the objects restored their images without interruption, and neither the image of the box nor that of the bed was ever used up. He opened his mouth. Looking at the gums — Kalb didn't know the epithelium they were made of, but the flesh glistened enchantingly. On an impulse, he decided also to try out the sensitivity of his skin and made contact with the tabletop. Just then a glass fell to the floor releasing a sound that had been hidden within its structure.

KALB leaned back in his chair. He felt his shoulder-bones. The menu was laid before him. But Kalb had no money. The waiter's sleeve brushed his hand. Kalb was on his own. His observations accumulated. The waiter's suit was black. The determinacy of appearances and processes hovered threateningly, waiting to be recognized. He was silent. The words grew like ulcers in his head. At last he seized his opportunity to disappear inconspicuously.

H E LAY in his bed. The blanket with the pattern of huge leaves slipped off onto the floor. He sprang up and held his head over the washbasin. He examined his vomit and recognized a mélange of remnants from his meal.

A JAR OF marmelade stood on the windowsill in Kalb's room. In the jelly's transparency were suspended golden shreds suggestive of fibrous fruit. Light-corpuscles spilled over the writing desk and struck the floor like dough. Without interruption images wiped across his retina.

THE FURNITURE van pulled up. It looked lifted from a de Chirico painting. Kalb stood around in his room. Words and noises were accompanied by their echoes. Kalb pulled out an empty drawer. Where the armoire had stood a precise geometrical stain could be seen. On Kalb's lip a fever blister was forming. A muted racket came up from the street below. Kalb seated himself on the sunlight spread over the floor. He felt the fever blister with the tip of his tongue. The movers hauled Kalb's belongings down the steps and over the flagstones in front of the house.

S LOWLY dusk fell. A little Pekinese stared out of the window. The butcher unloaded bloody carcasses. One passer-by had a pointy face and centimeter-thick lenses in his glasses which made the eyes underneath look too small.

THEY'RE ALL IDIOTS in love with classification, thought Kalb to himself, looking out the window over the city rooftops.

H E'D OPENED the book of anatomy and studied the reproductions awhile indifferently. Later he had gone to the tavern in order to eat. When he had gone back out on the street, the young woman had accosted him. Kalb went with her. In the lobby of the hotel there was a cash register painted blue. The concierge laid the key on the table. The young woman knew the way (of course) and went ahead eagerly. Shortly thereafter she showed Kalb two flat breasts. A handtowel and a bar of soap were laid out next to a washbowl decorated with flowers. Kalb stood up. He asked the young woman to put her clothes back on. He watched her dress. Only when the young woman walked to the door did he tuck in his shirt and follow suit.

CLOUDS WITH opalescent edges, made iridescent by the light's refraction through minute droplets of water, hung poised above Kalb's head. Kalb inspected the tireless activity of nature's machine attentively.

KALB had seen, for example, the following:
1. a woman with a bicycle hitched up to a two-wheeled wooden cart. The wooden cart was occupied by water-tubs filled with flowers.
2. a car, full of flowers.
3. a messenger in business attire on a bicycle with a wreath around his shoulder.
Kalb waded through these three-dimensional images. Events were broadcast live in his head.

D REAM — first Kalb's hand. Then the fingers. Kalb is in a raincoat. The floorboards shudder as if filmed by a hand-held camera. Children romp about at the head of the stairs. Down the stairs hops the tennisball. Kalb briskly stepped aside. The window offered a view of a hunched woman watering her flowers with an iron watering-can. On close examination he found that the windowpanes were grimy. Her hand is cold. Her hand is lovely. He leaves the house. In front of the house there is a phonebooth. A hair is suddenly sprouting from his neck! His stomach emitted sounds of digestion. His body must remain with him somehow and with him cross the street. He greeted the assistant Dr. Klopcic. The ocean of air weighed heavily upon him. A white arrow on the wall indicated the way. Kalb reacted like a compass-needle. He hurried up the stairs, crossed the balcony and entered the poorly-lit office. On the desk stood a balance, whose scales trembled as Kalb closed the door behind him. A bell jar, empty, stood beside it. Along the shelves stood rows of phials with handwritten labels. Under each phial was affixed a plaque with a number. Kalb was overcome by a fierce temptation to pry off a numbered plaque. Just then a hidden door opened and a bald-headed fellow sporting glasses asked what Kalb wanted.

A SOUND made Kalb start. Still half asleep, he had the impression of someone letting the door fall shut behind him. There: through the wall he heard a stranger coughing. Then it stopped abruptly. Kalb waited for the coughing to resume, but all remained still. Perhaps the man had choked on his cough? In his mind's eye Kalb saw the other room and the strange man suspended belly-up, midair, like a dead fish.

KALB opened the window. The sky was yellow like a lemon. The leaves were yellow like primroses. The handkerchief was yellow like a sunflower. The bicycle was yellow like egg-yolk. The shoes were yellow like urine. The wallpaper was yellow like parchment. The tooth was yellow like a canary.

H E ENTERED the tavern. A man drank out of a tea-glass, from which poked a spoon. His pupils split open and Kalb caught a glimpse of his brain through the pupil-fissures. Then his body, which of course consisted chiefly of water, was washed away, or vaporized, and where he had stood by the counter there was nothing left but a stubbed out cigarette.

KALB went back outside. The mail truck left a streak of exhaust. The birds dragged colorful vapor trails behind them. These vapor trails paused in the air without dissolving. Just as naturally, the fireplug continuously emitted the color red and pumped it into the air. Kalb settled himself on a stool in a snackbar. He considered his medication's circling trail through his body.

HE LOOKED ABOUT for a barber. At last he found a small, old-fashioned shop. He went in. The door slamming interrupted a conversation between the man perched on the barber-stool and the blond woman cutting his hair. The woman had just finished the job when Kalb — having pulled off his jacket — was ready to take a seat in the waiting room. Kalb took his place on the barber stool. He glanced at himself in the mirror. The mirror was splotched all over. The woman, exuding eau-de-cologne, asked Kalb what he wanted. She stood under the neon lights and pulsed with a pale glow. Kalb's sensory organs sucked up against her like octopus arms. The white plastic towel was tied around his throat. Kalb felt the woman's hands. On the porcelain stand stood small flasks, bottles, vessels, a can of hair gel. He sat silently and listened to the chatter of the scissors. When the hairdresser was done he paid and went back out into the open air. His neck itched from the tiny hairs that had slipped, despite the plastic towel, down his nape. He undid the top button of his shirt. He found himself in front of a gateway, and becoming curious, stepped closer so he could survey the entire courtyard. It was a place for washing cars. A crate of fruit was lifted out of the back of a car and set out on the asphalt. He turned and walked back to the barber shop.

A STREET-CLEANING machine was suddenly advancing on him. It crawled straight toward him with a high-pitched keening sound, as though it expected — sure of its prey — to roll slowly over him. Kalb pressed himself against the wall of the house. He stared at the machine, hypnotized. He felt the close warmth it emitted as it drove by him.

H E TRUDGED on for a bit. His lungs wheezed. His brain, the time-collapsing machine, piloted Kalb over the sidewalk.

ON THE WAY home he passed by a brightly lit window. Through the narrow slit between the tattered curtains he could clearly make out a man and a woman in carnal embrace. A cold lust of superiority gripped him so fiercely he couldn't tear his gaze away. Suddenly the man turned toward the window and stared at Kalb with crazed eyes, wordless, his mouth open.

HIS HAND touched the handrail running up along the stairs. He heard the landlady's dog barking from the darkness. He stopped still and breathed cautiously, without knowing why, as though he were being shadowed and must not betray his presence with the slightest sound. He climbed the stairs a little further. He observed that his trousercuffs were swaying back and forth.

H IS GLANCE plunged in a nose-dive over the sidewalk. On the ground lay a crumpled cigarettepack. A bit later schoolchildren stormed out onto the street. The cheeks of one child were streaked with tears, he looked absurd in a way, mainly because of his sailor suit. Kalb was silent. The child looked fearfully up at him regardless. Kalb left the child where he was. He walked into the school. In the hall, posters with illustrations of various fruits and flowers were fixed to the wall with explanatory titles. He went back out to the street. The child stood on the street with his head bowed. The sunlight beat down soundlessly upon the street. In a parked car a woman sat. She studied Kalb suspiciously. Kalb stopped and said something to the child. The child showed no reaction. He took a bill from his pocket and offered it to the child. At this point the woman rolled down the car window and watched Kalb with a look that said she was just about to say something to him. Kalb returned the bill to his pocket, but stood by for a bit. The woman kept an eye on him, but never actually spoke. Finally the child turned and shuffled off. Kalb went in the opposite direction. He paid no further attention to the woman in the car. He passed by a flowerstand. He inhaled deeply. He imagined he was a detective. For a brief moment he was mirrored in a stranger's sunglasses.

CHAINS OF imperceptible electric impulses material-ized and flitted off in Kalb's head. Things took form before his eyes, the reduced images of objects flowed along, were recognized, assimilated by association and organized into systems.

THE BOX lay open. On the inside lid of the box a bundle of neckties lay in view. At the bottom of the box there was dirty laundry. Kalb lounged back in the chair. He wore clean shoes. He was smoking a cigarette. His skin segregated him like insulating tape from the outside world.

H OW DID KALB endure the inconclusive events in his brain? The word-fragments that were caught incessantly by his ear, his absorption of idiosyncratic time, bits of incidents, snippets of events? What made him suffer through this uninterrupted series of fragments? What made him experience these agonizing circumstances as normal?

THE STREET-NAMES appeared before him like ghosts. Plaster fell from the houses. He entered the office supply shop. He bought a dozen envelopes and several postage stamps and put the stamps inside the envelopes. He handed over the money and left the store.

THE GOLD of musical instruments glared from the window-display. He buried his fists in his jacket. His lips were red. His lips were odd skins. He asked where the toilet was. His pants bunched around his thighs, his buttocks were bare. He masturbated and left the stall. On the sink lay a razorblade. The light was so fine, so artfully scattered, such a downy-soft and gentle, such a round smooth texture, that he was deeply moved. He stood on the bridge and stared at the river. The wind seeped into his clothing. . . The people were plasma membranes that collapsed and lay scattered about, like ketchup.

THE FROG-HEADED stranger turned his head after walking past. Immediately Kalb recognized the lymphoid sarcoma on his throat. The Politzer Process (Adam Politzer, Otologist, Vienna 1835-1920) is something else altogether, in fact it is a so-called air douche, i.e. an air injection by rubber ball through one nostril and Eustachian tube into the middle ear, while the other nostril is plugged and the nasal-pharyngeal passage is closed up by swallowing movements or humming. Kalb spat. He produced 1-2 liters of saliva per day (saliva possesses slightly bactericide characteristics: pH 5-8, specific weight 1002-1012). The sky itself had broken open and become black and gangrenous, then started to discharge fluids. The man with the frog-head had disappeared. Kalb took off his jacket and hung it carefully on a clotheshook. The woman watched him with huge, inflamed eyeballs. She had something of the occult about her. She shoved the cup of coffee across the table to him. The sugarcube disappeared into the coffee. Little bubble-blisters. He breathed against the windowpane, so that it fogged up.

THE WOMAN let him into the room. Kalb sat down on the bed, which sagged under his weight. The woman had melancholy eyes. The room looked as though it had pests nesting in the cracks. Left on the nightstand was a piece of half-eaten cheese someone had forgotten. There was not the slightest trace of an expression to be read off Kalb's features. He sat there like an ameoba. His body was soft and silky. The leg-muscles twitched. She lay on the bed, a purple sea-creature. Kalb was wearing all black. He felt his temples. He felt his hair. Small change jingled in his jacket when he laid it over the back of the chair. His nerve endings protruded forward out of his skin, millions of infinitesimal wounds.

FLOWERS, NO, plucked, shoved her tongue in his mouth, shattered, blood, went then over to the other and was already however in the window up high by the ceiling and was always already in the glowing-white hard and cracked gums, the bones beneath, had knocked over or jostled, rounded upon, then hat in the other hand, the necktie...eh...knocked over...eh...was definitely, was not in the least, no.

ON THE PLATE lay a plum. The bottle uttered a noise, when its cork was pulled out; he pulled his handkerchief out and dusted off the armchair before he sat down. Inside the plum was an elliptical plum-pit. Kalb's lips were instantaneously tugged upward into a smile. His bladder burned. Was that a knock at the door? Were the walls bending in? He had smoked too much. That crack in the ceiling. The burn-mark on the table-cloth. The remnants of dinner on the tablecloth. Through the wall he heard the drone of a vacuum cleaner. DEPICTION: He unbuttoned his shirt at the collar. He untied his shoelaces. He opened his eyes. END OF DEPICTION.

HE STARED into the palm of his hand. He opened the sardine tin. He uncoiled the elastic bandage from his ankle. Slowly the drops of water ballooned outward from the end of the faucet. In the botanical atlas there was an image of a huge green plant, with green wrinkles, green skin, green flesh. When he fetched the bottle from the refrigerator, frost-drops rolled over the glass. The flowerbed, several meters wide, was already completely white. There, over the surface, the perfume froze. He turned the gas-knob on and held the match over the burner. He leafed through his book. His toes had reddened and swollen. Since the chairlegs were uneven, he teetered with every movement. He leaned forward, sliced the lemon and beheld the symmetry of its cross-section. He squeezed the lemon over the sardines. He coughed: his bronchial tubes contracted, the alveolae quivered in miniature convulsions, and the cough tumbled down the window and crackled on the land-lady's eardrums.

H E MARVELED at the clarity of a common Schnapps glass, the bizarrely metaphysical humor that it was capable of activating within him. As though balanced by an acrobat it stood on the table, and for a short while sabotaged his reason. With enchanted revulsion he placed it on the floor. Fatigue made him lose his balance a bit. He took a step forward. How could this Schnapps glass, upon accidentally appearing within his field of vision, manipulate his reason and will to the extent that he was made to carry out actual *movement*? But wasn't the chair on which he sat also a mystery? Or the doorframe? In his head deadly night-shade bloomed, numbed his brain, made it limp like dead cuttlefish. He went down and ordered two pig-kidneys at the butcher's. The butcher wrapped them up in newspaper and pressed them into Kalb's hand, cold meat. Kalb pocketed them. The world outside sat astride his brain like a jockey and tightened the reins. A huge red lobster posed in one of the shop-windows. It stared into nothingness with small black eyes. With each new instant Kalb burned through another of time's exposures. Were they phantoms assaulting him, was it reality? The man in the blue hat was the celebrated Utopian Seuter, who got muscle-cramps in his jaw when he laughed. Kalb accompanied him a short distance, but had no answer to Seuter's urgent question. At last he took his leave. Kalb saw him enter the drugstore. He dug for the meat in his coat-pocket. With a vulgar sensation of limpness and cold, reality answered Kalb's touch. Kalb took his hand back out of his coatpocket. He felt the weight of the pig-kidneys pulling his jacket down.

KALB relished the strangeness that was unleashed within him when he walked along and associated his perception with the sensation of the animal organs in his pocket. The man before him, for example, was a sea-monster, a huge white jellyfish. If he wanted to, Kalb could walk right through him, as through some ornament on reality he'd dreamed up. His line of vision was slippery and objects escaped from him without his being able to account for their meaning.

SUDDENLY AN electric surge shot through him. Pure physics. Epileptic frame-rate. The sun hung low like a chandelier. He held up the paper bills, just checking. Infrared paper, indigo-blue sheen, ultramarine watermark. His flesh sagged. His glands twitched or vibrated or it started with his cerebellum. He leaned against a tree. His consciousness was just like a current-transformer. The weather lowered itself and lay about in slack poses. Kalb let his senses wash whatever items appeared before him: trees, houses, pedestrians, vehicles. His spleen nestled sinuously in his body, busily producing lymphocytes, antibodies, and the like. When the same stimulus activated different patches of his retinae, objects appeared to have moved.

OF COURSE TIME showered his perception as well. Iron oxide had corroded and magnetized Kalb's fillings. Pollution poured from his tonsils. "My dear woman, it seems you have a hole in your stocking!" Kalb laughed like a refrigerator. The woman looked down, startled. He entered the telegraph office. Ink spots on the wall that looked like little fish. He stood up and went out. He emitted the scent of violets, of Beethoven, of mirrors, of cloves. He stopped to urinate on the outside wall of the house.

THEN A TRULY shit-faced albino with red eyes came along, was well-behaved like Thomas Mann and stepped to the side so as to let Kalb by. Kalb perceived that he had an intelligent look about him. (That reassuring effect, when things were consistently found within their appropriate contexts!) — His face was completely made of quince jelly. Having stored up printer's ink in his mouth, he blew a speech bubble in the air. Kalb allowed himself to fall into conversation with him. He went back to the Anatomy Building. (One floor above were the laboratories of the Physiological Institute where they cut off frogs' heads with shears, after having first grabbed them by the hind legs and hit their heads against the sink.) He enjoyed his hallucinatory angle, the view of glass chemistry equipment in the storefront display. With an elegant movement of his fin, Kalb changed direction and shot under the parchment foliage of the chestnuts.

AGAIN HE FELT around for the pig kidneys in his coat pocket. And already with every fraction of a second, rushing Tesla-currents washed up snapshots before him. The music rinsed out his ears with sharp acidic blood and the blood ran out his ears. His eyes gleam. Varnished glass. A vein vibrates soft pink-violet out of the back of his hand. His spittle freezes, the salt eats away at his tearducts, his tongue swells. But each cause continually brought about a parade of different effects. The minutes had been splashing, ever since the morning, upon the same spot on his head.

BEHIND THE NEXT corner stood the pensioner Schuller, one arm in a sling, a face like a somnambular grub, gasping for oxygen. Kalb splintered the thin layer that had frozen over his thoughts, surfaced and found himself pitched over at the feet of old Mr. Schuller, who paused, disconcerted. Having nothing to say for himself, he brushed off his trousers.

KALB piloted Kalb gently between the looming houses. In the sunlight he showed his emerald beauty like a great anemone, his tentacles undulating, ornamented with a carotin pigment, loose in the air, a glinting organic particle of decomposed matter. He ordered a plate of salad and the meaty cup of his belly closed and opened itself.

H IS ENVIRONMENT provided uninterrupted stimulation. His weak ankle was well-bandaged.
In the sideboard he located the teapot.

HIS LANDLADY'S door was ornamented with colored glass. He knocked. The lady opened it. Kalb remained in the doorway. He watched, while the dog devoured the pig kidneys he'd thrown him. Then the landlady stepped so close to him that he could see her glistening pink scalp through the thin covering of hair.

H E TOOK THE TEAPOT from the stove. On the street a little girl went by, a bow in her hair, a violin under her arm. As she walked, the girl pulled her skin over her head, a long bloody sheet, and stood in glittering splendor in the gutter. In his thoughts Kalb, as a kingfisher, shot out at the girl and pecked tiny morsels of meat out of her living body.

THE CHESSBOARDS in the park were still set up, but there was no sign of the players. Kalb sought the nearest café, where, among the antiques, plush sofas and armchairs, porcelain vases, a piano and gaudy tapestries, he found the chessplayers he was looking for. Kalb noted the nervous fingers: after gripping the plain wooden figures they hit the timer loudly, or they performed grasping movements mid-air before they could decide on a move. Dispassionately, neutrally, he directed his gaze at the players. A hat lay on the table, next to a dessert spoon. One of the players made an "I"-statement, referring to himself. The others had no trouble understanding him. Kalb felt his cavity with his tongue. The player that had spoken suddenly appeared as a negative image, but no one said a word about it. He sat in the armchair like an apparition, like a white current of light. Kalb understood this to be a mathematical process, bodily algebra, a physiological integral equation. He was alone with his bottles of medication and his intestines. The other one lay on the table like an oversized leaf-shaped liver fluke parasite, sponging nutrients from the velvety bile-ducts of the surrounding onlookers with whose blood he nourished himself. It was luxurious, the way his spiracle would clamp shut. His eyes protruded with his opponent's every move, growing into two swollen mucus-valves. His fingernail was made of concentric layers of mother-of-pearl, ears silently flittered, strange flutter-funnels. If someone irritated him, he emitted a blinding, cloudy phosphor that paralyzed his audience. Kalb walked back to the park. An apple with a bite missing lay on the chesstable. Its bitten flesh had already turned brown.

LATER HE followed a woman with whom he'd spoken in the course of wandering around. Her face was bloated, her pregnant body misshapen. She closed the curtains. Kalb's member was a benumbed needle of ice. He paid with a cloud of purple postage stamps that spun up to the ceiling in a gust of wind and fluttered slowly back down onto the woman's swollen stomach.

H E HAILED a taxi. For a little while he allowed himself to be chauffeured around with no destination. He climbed out. He turned the doorknob to his room. He groped for the lightswitch. The bottle of ink fell to the floor. It bloomed in a blue stain. Kalb stood paralyzed before it, a secret agent with an attack of angina pectoris. In a vase an orchid had burst open, innocently baring its magnificent giblets. He sat down at the table and spooned up a soft-boiled egg. He left the hollowed-out eggshell lying on the table.

I N THE EARLY MORNING he went back out onto the street. The café had only just opened. The air tasted sweet. He accidentally brushed against the ice-cold marble table-top. He thought of the eggshell on the table in his room. His reflections were laid out in artful counterpoint to the streaming current of reality. Through the glass pane he could see an old-fashioned corset-shop in the window opposite, in which a lone bustier hung from a metal mannequin in the otherwise empty display, decorated with lace. He enjoyed the unique musical score of accidental perceptions.

I N ORDER to stimulate his fantasies, he walked to the pawnbroker's. The street ran down a hill. In the delicatessen, meat and mock sausages were set out on display. An usher was airing out the cinema and spraying Lysol over the open seats.

HE FELT THE NAKED flesh of his palate. Ozone flickered. He spun around and let his eyes pulse. Meteorology proved its superconductivity by dispersing the humidity. A hot day. He stood before the pawn-broker's. Time beat down against him, slowly seeped through him. The irrational turbulence in his head manifested itself in an aneurysm, which grew like an amniotic sac out of his skull and, when it had filled with helium, resembled a floating bell made of glass. He pawned his pocketwatch. He was weary, like a side-walk detective. The fever nested in his shirt, in his shoes, in his bones, in his banknotes, in his alcohol-breath, in the pocket edition of Edgar Allan Poe stories he'd bought with the money for his pawned watch. He stopped in at the flophouse. The linens smelled like vinegar. He read the posted regulations. He saw a passerby with a pockmarked face. He followed him to the cemetery. He watched as he filled a can with water and slowly disappeared among the gravestones. He waited. He leafed through the book, he read a few lines. No one. He returned the book to his pocket. In a zinc bucket were rotting plants, the remnants of flowers, pink tissuepaper. Then he saw the man with the pockmarked face walking toward him.

THE MAN turned left. Kalb's brain revealed itself to be a mimosa-like filter. He followed the pockmarked man like a morphine addict. A feeling of strangeness overcame him. Just as suddenly as he'd begun his pursuit, he broke off. He sat on one of the benches along the street and read the story of "Dr. Thaer and Prof. Fedders." He couldn't read the story to its end, as before long he felt the cold of the bench through his trousers; his thoughts, however, wouldn't leave what he'd read. As he walked he began to read on. Reading the book was now made more difficult, since at every step the book's pages shook and his eyes lost their place. He kept stopping so he could finish a sentence or a line. When he had read the story, he walked back to the bookstore and exchanged the book, conveying the impression that he'd wanted to give the book as a gift to someone who — as it turned out — already owned it.

HE WENT TO the nearby public library. At the coatcheck he was asked to leave his jacket. The light fell milky through the dim glass ceiling in the reading room. The light-globes projecting from the walls on curved iron hooks looked like bulging eyeballs hanging from the nerve fibers of a gigantic bloodless fish. Next to the entrance sat a librarian sharpening a pencil. For unexplained reasons Kalb began to take an interest in his voice, how it would sound — and how would he react to this or that word? Kalb approached him, but because of his prolonged silence he could only manage a whisper. The librarian riffled through a bundle of borrow-slips, answered Kalb that the work he wanted was unavailable, and returned to twisting his pencil.

KALB sat. The light-globes appeared to him as magical glass creatures in a cold world of mechanical objects. Should he get up, stroll back through the library and retrieve his jacket? Or would it be better to remain here in his chair, at the mercy of his thoughts, until a long enough interval had separated him from what had happened, and his sangfroid was restored? He stood up with a start. He walked back between the long green wooden tables. At the coatcheck he requested his jacket.

A T THE ALL-NIGHT theater he'd happened upon, he purchased a ticket. The usher directed him to a half-filled row. He sat down with a stranger to his right, but nobody to his left. He changed his wallet from the right to the left jacket pocket. (He wanted to be sure that he couldn't be robbed.) In the meantime he had already laid his coat over the seat-back in front of him. The movie was about a photographer who became ensnared in a murder in an unexpected manner.

AFTER THE SHOW he staggered out of the cinema, his brain iridesced dark purple. He paused before the sign

Dr. S. Hoff
Specialist in Skin- and Sexually Transmitted Diseases

momentarily. He entered the building and sat down on a staircase. The film ran through his head. He climbed up the steps to the doctor's office. He rang. Directly there followed a buzzing sound. Kalb pushed against the door. It gave way and he found himself in a waiting room in which two men and a woman were sitting around. Rubber tubes ran out of their noses, their eyes glistened like pink cartilage. Again the film passed through Kalb's mind. A nurse approached Kalb, her features devastated by injections of paraffin, her hands, however, in sharp contrast, tender and smooth like Chinese ivory — "Do you have a health insurance card?" Kalb answered that he had only rung out of curiosity, and left, before things could get any worse.

H E TOOK the streetcar to a distant district of the city. During the ride he stared out at the street. He fingered a strangely insensitive gland under his ear. He got off at a stop. Over a timber fence he saw a man flaying a hare. Kalb watched the man until he was finished. Now the hare hung red and naked from the bough, like a newborn child. The unforeseen spit out new images continuously.

O N THE RIGHT appeared the gloomy buildings of the lung hospital. A fellow in a hospital gown stood on the gravel path. Kalb examined him out of the corner of his eye, all the while pretending not to notice him. The fellow walked abreast of Kalb on the other side of the fence. Before the main entrance he turned and walked out over the lawn. Kalb followed him. He entered the next building and spied through the door left ajar. The door led into a lecture hall, in which there were a great quantity of chairs set up, which with their identical seat-backs and tall legs were configured in a surreal pattern. He sat down. After several minutes he felt an agonizing disquiet and left the lecture hall through the open door.

TOWARD MIDDAY he walked by a tavern. The kitchen window had been left open. On the table lay a bloody liver; various vegetables, bearing a vague resemblance to human organs, were scattered over a wooden board. He imagined he was examining the remains of a gruesome crime.

H E DIDN'T CARE to be alone any longer. He redeemed his watch at the pawnbroker's. He sought out the pregnant woman's rooms. He knocked. No one opened. He walked back down the steps and waited in front of the house. He went to the park that ran along the other side of the street, came back again — still no one opened. He pulled out his watch. The pocketwatch showed the same time as his wristwatch. First thing this morning he had synchronized them. He held them to his ears. He wanted to ascertain whether the ticking sounds overlapped one another. To his surprise the ticks coincided in one phase, then fell out of step in the next. Suddenly he lost interest and put the pocketwatch away. He went back to his room. He studied the pigeons, who plunged like heavy objects past his window into the depths without making a sound. One heard only a gentle crackle when they spread their wings to break the fall. On a low-lying rooftop Kalb could see from his window, the wind had blown hundreds of yellow leaves. Now and then a handful was driven in a gust over the eaves and tossed pirouetting into the air.

H E SAT DOWN on his bed. He laid the cigarette-carton before him on the blanket. He stared at it until it was completely foreign to him. His consciousness lay beneath a disorderly current of perceptions and thoughts. The furniture floated freely and effortlessly in space. Was that the category of Matter? Would it only manifest itself in a jolting flash? It was as though he were reading a detailed account of his dreams, as transcribed by himself.

HIS FLICKERING drunkenness turned his gaze to the orchid, which had begun to wilt. He topped it up with fresh water. From a disorganized pile of books he pulled a volume of Baudelaire. The sun trickled through the window.

THE PHYSIOGNOMY of objects touched him, made him forget the heavy air, implicated him in a conspiracy. How small the room was! The box's key appeared disproportionately larger than the box. He was the pathologist who used his eyes for scalpels. He thought of the day in February when he had suffered his first bout of migraines. The orchid in the meantime had decayed syphilitically from the oxygen and with every tenth of a second sagged further down into itself. His feeling for all matter confronting him continued to be a conspiratorial one. He gazed with growing awe, for example, upon the magical parquet molding, in which cold air was always trapped.

H E COLLECTED perceptions, like a ragman.

THE WINE WAS fragrant. His cobalt vision pierced space in the form of two needle-points. The billiard table, a cadmium color, was bulging, the ivory balls struck one another with a dull knock. The maître d' placed a glass in front of one of the patrons. Kalb instantly mimicked the meaningful swoop of the waiter's arm-movement while knocking one back. His mind worked, wide-awake and with wide-open focus, while his body dreamed. He apprehended the particles around him and pasted them together in his brain. He fixed his gaze on the cash-register by the counter until the cast-iron shell burst open and the machine-parts the keys set in motion were revealed. Kalb hallucinated reality.

H E SAT DOWN on a chair. With this bodily movement the watery fluid in his balancing organs was disturbed and sent the minutest stimuli to the inner ear and the tiny sensitive hairs of his vestibular apparatus. This was quite pleasant. He repeated the motion. The billiard table glided into his field of vision and with it the fruit that stood in a bowl, as though lacquered, on one of the coffeehouse tables.

A FEELING OF equilibrium between waking and dreaming had taken possession of him. He stepped over to another patron's table and asked him to hand him that glass. The man looked at him, puzzled, and reached for the glass. The moment he did Kalb boxed his ears. The fellow sprang up indignantly. Kalb made no motion to flee or even to resume his ear-boxing. Someone tossed the bill on his table. Kalb paid. The patron whose ears he'd boxed was calling for the police but the waiter had already dragged Kalb out the door and shoved him into the open air.

H E FOUND HIMSELF in the street. In his imagination he saw himself on a bleached dageurreotype by the windowpane of a coffeehouse on which an ad for a French aperitif company was printed in gigantic letters. His consciousness telegraphed the pose to his limbs. He let his thoughts manipulate him at all times. His skull burned. He was able clearly to project the episode of the ear-boxing before his mind's eye, as clearly as if he were a disinterested party observing a stranger, without even losing the sequence of proper reactions to this act of violence, from shock to consternation and disgust, even though it was of course he who had caused the incident.

H E ROAMED ABOUT. He walked into a restaurant. The electric light bulbs exploded. The plates exploded. The windowpanes exploded. He sat down. He was afraid of pointlessly squandering the voltage of his brain. The blood retreated from his hands and dammed up in his wrists.

A FAT MIDDLE-AGED woman nodded to him. He sat down at the woman's table. The woman dropped a hand down to his knee. Her features were disguised in skin. The hand pressed his knee. He gripped the table's edge painfully. He could see the marble cake disappear down the woman's oral cavity, he watched her jaw chew as it drained the sweet flavor out of a mouthful of cake, so as to communicate an aura of sensuous pleasure. "Keep me company?" The woman had stood up. On the way she asked Kalb's name. Kalb accepted the invitation for a cognac. He sat down upon the sofa. His hands shoved themselves up under her dress. The woman began hastily to tear off her clothes. Kalb removed his tie. He felt the woman's wild, convulsing thighs on his hips. He enjoyed the disordery images which emerged in his imaginary world. He thought about robbing the woman, rummaging through the wardrobe, hiding the stolen money. Exhausted, he sank down on his side.

U PON LEAVING his room, he turned and — instead of going down the steps, as usual, and walking out the front door — climbed up several flights. He glanced out the hall window at the street below. He glimpsed the trees, forms made of black bark, fanned by the yellow smoke-plumes of the fall leaves, small thickets that seemed to have shot up to euphoric heights, then burst — the shattered fragments clung to the branches like parchment auricles. Following a sudden impulse, he knocked on the nearest door. The door was torn open and a rake-thin frame with amphibian eyes stood before him. It wore a suit of threadbare clothing, a waistcoat buttoned up crookedly, baggy trousers, a necktie tied so carelessly around his neck that one could see part of the rubberband with which it was fastened.

Yes?

The man's cold tone and resolute mien shattered Kalb's poise.

He had the extraordinary honor, said Kalb, soon that was, to be a neighbor of a sort...

So? the man interrupted him — and?

...and so he would like to get some pointers regarding the customs of the house...

Customs? What customs? Who was he, in any case?

So he wasn't the one to come to for this sort of information? Then he must have gotten the floors completely mixed up! So he wasn't Mister...er...Tarski?

Tarski? There was no Mister Tarski here! What did he want!

Then he must have gotten all mixed up, answered Kalb, excused himself and feigning infirmity began to stump slowly back down the stairs.

III. Morphology

ONE DAY KALB fell into conversation with a drunkard on problems of metaphysics, which the man tried to explain using Newtonian axioms. It emerged that he lived with a crumpled old woman, who kept a dog out of distrust. She opened the door and began immediately to speak. Her teeth fluttered in her mouth like autumn leaves; drops of blood dripped like poppy-blossoms through her slack veins. Kalb touched her with his vision, and his eyes hurt from the contact.

THE DRUNKARD asked Kalb to accompany him to a laundromat. The stone floor shimmered with a sulphurous liquid. In one corner a bundle of umbrellas leaned together in a jumble. Kalb gazed intently at his feet and shoes. A nun rustled by him wearing a rustling nun's habit of black holy water. They went back to the house, where the elderly lady was sitting with her dog on a sofa awaiting a visitor. Kalb wished that, instead of his shirts and underwear, he could pull out an amputated child's leg and offer it to the dog to devour, while the drunkard wrapped his naked torso with iodine bandages. However, nothing of the kind occurred.

INSTEAD, the drunkard was looking for a box of matches. The ink-colored bags under his eyes drooped halfway down his cheeks. Kalb watched a fly traversing an opened, abandoned letter. It reminded him, to his astonishment, of the clopping of horse-hooves, which he was unable to make sense of and immediately forgot again.

O N THE SAME DAY he happened to make the acquaintance of an engineer in the wine bar through a telepathic process, a man perhaps in his forties. As their conversation was just beginning the proprietress, Frau Riegler, placed a bunch of wet plastic violets (presumably just held under faucet-water) on the table and Kalb could see the stalks through the glass, and the pearly air-bubbles beading along the stems. Outside it had begun to rain. Kalb imagined he perceived the scent of violets. The blond hairdresser slipped into his brain — her hands had been similarly scented.

H E WATCHED the engineer with multifaceted eyes, a surrealist insect that darted with an imperceptibly light tingling over the engineer's clothes and skin.

THE DISTILLED FRUIT reposed unctuously in jars. The streetcars dreamed gently and silently outside the windows, upon which birds, murdered by morse code, eavesdropped on the hum of electric sewing machines. Pictures fell from the wall, clocks came to a standstill at the very moment kinsfolk passed from life into death. Steps swam along time's sine curve and twisted in a gyrating motion and turned themselves in ferris wheels fixed in place like the pulsing water sprinklers between the flowerbeds of the suburban gardens. Kalb put into action the dropping of a bouillon cube (with a picture of a white cow) into the purple pot. The north pole sent a current of icy wind across his skin. He saw the grand piano in the engineer's apartment approaching, monstrous and black. The piano-strings trembled. The seconds writhed and rolled over on the floor. In silence they began to devour the flowers. The cage was covered with a white sheet to prevent the parrakeet from being woken by the morning sunlight. Then he pulled the handkerchief off with a flourish and dragged it smoothly like a cello's bow over his forehead, and his bodily substance clung to it. In the early evening the engineer began to cry. The photographs glued into oval frames rocked lifelessly over his knees. In one of the photos Otto von Zeppelin, earnest and composed, looked into the objective lens of the gigantic, now (of course) no longer visible camera-box, with which the viewer's gaze or (if you prefer) pupil was aligned. This identification would always repeat itself, forever, with the regularity and calculability of a natural law.

IN THE EARLY MORNING, reeling through the still deserted streets, Kalb looked up at the leaves measuring their own revolutions and being washed over by the oxygen's foamy spray; they were constantly reawoken to twitching life by the buzz of the telephone wires. The sidewalk played his footsteps like a piano. Everything lay sleeping, only the bleary-eyed doctor with his shirtcollar open and his medical bag jingling, ran panting across the street, so he'd be in time to set up the music stand before his dying patient, and with virtuosic grip, coax the violin to sing.

HIS LUNGS dyed the litmus paper of his lips blue through their asthmatic bellows, or it was phenolphthalein which flowed through his bloodstream and conjured this ghastly poetry to his lips. He stood still to catch his breath.

N IGHT'S BUTTERFLY, the moth, had landed on his
sleeve: a familiar creature, widespread throughout
Central Europe under the name "Blue-banded
Underwing." Kalb took no notice of it. His urbane brain
cut the most magnificent capers, as, chloroformed by
fatigue, it directed its incoming perceptions along the
most absurd paths and enjoyed the utter senselessness
of its associations.

S TILL AFFLICTED with the corrupted images of exhaustion, which on the chessboard of his brain clashed against one another now in the strangest configurations, he fell into bed. The sounds of the waking day spun around in his ear and tore him for brief moments out of the depths of sleep. He dreamed of steam engines whose brass pedals caused mechanical birds to discourse on Socratic philosophy. A boy embroidered with sequins sat convulsed by a shivering fit on a kitchen chair. Was he this child, with the chalk-white even part through his hair, who appeared to him in his dream?

A PPALLED, he sat up, he cleaned his shoes, he placed the chair by the window.

THROUGH THE TELESCOPE of his isolation he examined the image of the street. Today's dream came in green and red. The elderly lady hauled a jug of milk along the sidewalk, overtook and tread upon her own shadow, which accompanied her anew immediately thereafter, on the other side of her body. THE MOST TEDIOUS DETAILS ARE THE MOST LIKE DREAMS. Two flies buzzed about angrily. He engaged them in psychic congress. He took the bowl of peaches out of the refrigerator. His teeth hurt with every bite. In the flowerpot plummet-weights were rusting. The seismograph registered rust-red curves on a sheet of graph paper. The paving-stones buckled up elastically, which made the pedestrians seem like gymnasts stomping on a rubber trampoline.

HE TOOK SEVERAL drops of medicine. His oral cavity was suddenly filled with a minty taste. Even the room smelled like menthol. When he looked at the windowseat, he saw his own left nostril, although his glance went right along the windowseat. Though the taste of mint grew weaker in his mouth, the menthol smell persisted, had dispersed itself through his room's interior due entirely to Kalb's thought process, and from this a feeling of coolness and order was everywhere reflected once more.

A STRANGER hurried by. Immediately afterward Time closed over the hurrying stranger in waves and swallowed him whole.

H E TORE HIMSELF away from the window. He saw himself now on the street, which was made solid by its stillness. Everything appeared to him as an absurd drapery. The boulevards crossed one another, empty of pedestrians. Behind the walls of houses an accumulation of stuffy closets with bad lighting, full of people sleeping. The rain-green front door banged open and shut. Air-tremored curtains. Suddenly a bus drove by.

A GAIN the deadened panorama of the street enveloped him. A woman beat a red carpet.

KALB entered the tavern. He saw traces of beerfoam on the steel surface of the bar counter. In a corner was a small cast iron stove with a grotesquely long chimney. The rubber casing on the hostess's finger attracted his attention. On a hook hung the dailies. He believed he recognized the symptoms of sickness in himself, and felt a peculiar satisfaction.

IV. From the Notes for "The Will to Sickness"

THE CARETAKER stood on the sidewalk. He chose that moment to carve open his dog Bello, revealing his bowels. (The anatomical structures of such a man or a dog is really quite something.) Meanwhile the caretaker fastened a collar around Bello's neck and into the tavern they went, everyone turning to watch them come in.

The act of vomiting can be induced by the mucous membrane of the pharynx or by the stomach lining. But the taste and olfactory nerves can also initiate the process (or help it along) with the right sort of stimuli. A rather more mechanical, or chemical, stimulus in the central reflex quarter of the hindbrain produces *cerebral* vomiting.

Kalb, the flaneur.

The leaves on the trees had just now changed color, creatures fluttered and crawled about.

What is the clock? The clock is an adding machine. The clock is a symbol. The clock is a piece of jewelry.

Is it not peculiar that such an enormous creature as the whale sees the world through such a miniscule eye, and perceives sound through an ear that is smaller than that of a hare?

Kalb sat on the parkbench, equipped with his retinae, and tested reality. A man had a bandaid stuck to his forehead. Other than that, nothing was happening.

As long as Kalb studied the cat, she was present in his head, circling around in his brain, encouraging it to react to her image. But as soon as she crawled under the bed, she had as it were exited Kalb's head through his eyes.

The sun's angle of incidence averaged 26 degrees. North wind, 10 degrees celsius. The sounds from various wave-length-ranges. Kalb crossed the street.

Unexpectedly a ricochet of a visual image came flying toward him: a child on a tricycle. The images reverberated in Kalb's head. He closed his eyes to examine the figural echo.

The very same day, Kalb was introduced to the sensation of alarm that follows when one expects the elevator to travel upward but instead it sinks to the cellar.

The woman leaned forward, her breasts were plump. Her bodice was dirty. The woman rolled her stockings down. The electrical cord to the lightswitch had not been plastered over. On the inside of her thigh he can see the veins glisten. It is cold. There is no heater in the room. Kalb stepped toward the window and checked whether it was closed. He felt the cold that came in through the closed window. The curtains were worn threadbare. The carpet was small and dirty. It wasn't really a carpet at all, it was more of a bedside rug. In the woman's shoes you could see half a footprint. Kalb bent over her toes and examined her toenails. The skin on her buttocks was decorated with lots of small pustules. The sheet was cold. The woman had turned her face away and was staring at the floor. The curtains were hung from a brass rod. On the table one could see the circular mark of a glass. The woman smoked. She'd had a perm, and her hair was stiffly curled. She had a fur coat which hung from the clothes-hook on the inside of the door. The doorhandle was brass. It hung lopsided. The gloves lay like dead skin on the armchair.

111

He knew that his eyes were glinting. His glance swung around weighted like lead. He sat down in the pastry shop. The waitress had dirty fingernails. It didn't bother him. The waitress ran around. An electric clock hung on the wall. There was nothing new for him to uncover. There was nothing special about the waitress. Her outfit had no folds or pleats to speak of. Even the dog in the corner was nothing special. Outside the streetcar drove by. He smoked a cigarette. He paid. He went out to the street.

Someone spoke to him: This man had a bloated face. He asked for directions. Kalb followed him. The man entered a backyard. He glanced furtively around. Then he opened the trashbin and rummaged through the garbage. The carpet-beating rack had rotted through, the wood was all black. The man slunk back again. Kalb stepped into the wall-niche.

Everything was filled with honey.

Kalb stood up. The things he thought were always the same. The whole day he thought the same things as always.

All this, it's just like in the panopticon, said Kalb to himself.

He put the coins in the Coke machine. One of the coins slipped through and Kalb had to try with another coin.

He walked by an empty tennis court.

He wished he were an exhibitionist.

A single leaf hung from a tree.

Momentarily his face was concealed by cigarette smoke.

Kalb relished this disgust.

Saliva consists of water, inorganic salts, albumin, mucin, potassium, and the amylums of dissolved pytalin.

On the bed lay the ovaries.

From his nose he pulled a bloody handkerchief.

In the eprouvettes and cannulae deep-frozen straw-berries and liquid minerals frothed over the flames of a stearin candle.

The stimulation process in the sense-receptor cells and nerve-fibers is by nature electric. The encryption of the stimulus for the excitation-charge is the same in different sense organs. The manner of sensation depends upon which region of the brain the stimulant's message is carried to.

Kalb's body was flexible as wax and could be contorted into any conceivable posture. His plumage shone now blue-green, his back dazzled turquoise-blue, on his ear a rust-red marking, white stripe on the neck, white throat, underbelly shining reflective rust-red, long, powerful wedge-beak, feet coral-red.

The tea flowed through his mouth, his throat, his esophagus, and into his stomach.

Otherwise, collective appearances dominated the street.

Kalb's hair sprouted outward from its roots. Now his hairs were outside, and smooth as silk they covered the surface of his skin. Sometimes his sebaceous gland produced and discharged its lubricant too eagerly, and Kalb's hair clung, stringy and greasy, plastered to his skull.

A sleep-inducing dream-layer lay over all objects.

Biographical Note

It was in his early novellas that Gerhard Roth developed his "objective" prose, i.e. aggregates of particular impressions with a quasi-scientific emphasis on minute detail. The subjective narrator observes, notes, and produces thoughts. Synthesis eludes his capacities and perspective. The effect of this prose is surreal with an undertone of Angst that perceives anything as strange and menacing.

Born in 1942, in Graz, Austria, Roth studied to be a doctor (like his father), but dropped out and worked as a manager at the Graz Center for Statistics. In the late 1960s, he began to write and publish in the literary journal *manuskripte*, a mouthpiece for the literary group known as "Forum Stadtpark" (later renamed Grazer Autorenversammlung, or Graz Writers' Collective, where Peter Handke and Elfriede Jelinek also first made their mark).

By 1978, Roth had published three remarkable experimental novellas, *Die Autobiographie des Albert Einstein* (1972), *Der Ausbruch des Ersten Weltkrieg*s [The Outbreak of the First World War] (1972), our present *Der Wille zur Krankheit* (1973), as well as four novels, and received the first of his many literary awards (among them, the "Alfred-Döblin," "Marie-Luise-Kaschnitz," and "Bruno-Kreisky" prizes).

Over the next fifteen years, he continued to explore the Austrian psyche in genres ranging from children's books to screenplays, and, most impressively, in the seven volumes of *Die Archive des Schweigens*. This "Archive of Silence," which comprises a photographic anthology, a collection of essays, a biography and four novels, is widely considered Roth's masterpiece.

Roth (like the late Thomas Bernhard) is a political presence in his country and sees it as part of his role as a writer to make himself heard against the official silence or doublespeak that distorts the complexity of truths, whether concerning Austria or indeed the rest of the world.

Tristram Wolff graduated from Brown University in 2004. He lives in rural Vermont at present, and travels often. This translation is his first publication.

SELECTED BURNING DECK TITLES:

Walter Abish, *99: The New Meaning* (collage texts). 112 pp.
Tom Ahern, *The Capture of Trieste* (8 stories). 66 pp.
Anne-Marie Albiach, *A Geometry*, trans. K. & R. Waldrop. 26 pp.
Pierre Alferi, *OXO* (poetry), trans. Cole Swensen. 88 pp.
Beth Anderson, *Overboard* (poetry). 80 pp.
Rae Armantrout, *Precedence* (poetry). 48 pp.
Anthony Barnett, *Poem About Music*. 64 pp.
Mei-mei Berssenbrugge, *The Heat Bird* (poems). 64 pp.
Alison Bundy, *Duncecap* (stories). 128 pp.
Marcel Cohen, *The Peacock Emperor Moth*, trans. Cid Corman(stories). 112 pp.
Robert Coover, *The Grand Hotels (of Joseph Cornell)* (fiction). 64 pp.
Jean Daive, *A Lesson in Music*, trans. Julie Kalendek (poem). 64 pp.
Tina Darragh, *Striking Resemblance* (4 poems). 64 pp.
Michael Davidson, *The Landing of Rochambeau* (poems).80 pp.
Barbara Einzig, *Life Moves Outside* (short prose). 64 pp.
Elke Erb, *Mountains in Berlin*, selected and trans. R. Waldrop. 96 pp.
Patrick Fetherston, *The World Was a Bubble* (biography of Sir Francis
    Bacon, in verse with prose interruptions). 52 pp.
Susan Gevirtz, *Hourglass Transcripts* (poems). 70pp.
Peter Gizzi, *Artificial Heart* (poems). 96 pp.
Barbara Guest, *The Countess from Minneapolis*. 46 pp.
Ludwig Harig, *The Trip to Bordeaux*. trans. Susan Bernofsky. 104 pp.
Emmanuel Hocquard , *A Test of Solitude*, trans. R. Waldrop. 72pp.
Ernst Jandl, *reft and light*. A selection of poems with multiple
    translations by American poets. Ed. R. Waldrop. 112 pp.
Lisa Jarnot, *Some Other Kind of Mission* (poems). 112 pp.
Julie Kalendek, *Our Fortunes* (poems). 56 pp.
Janet Kauffman, *Five on Fiction* (fiction/theory). 64 pp.
Paol Keineg, *Boudica*, trans. Keith Waldrop (poem). 64 pp.
Damon Krukowski, *5000 Musical Terms* (poems). 28 pp.
Jessica Lowenthal, *as if in turning* (poems). 28 pp.
Elizabeth MacKiernan, *Ancestors Maybe* (novel). 160 pp.
Jackson Mac Low, *The Virginia Woolf Poems*. 44 pp.
Tom Mandel, *Realism* (prose and verse). 80 pp.
Jennifer Martenson, *Xq28* (poem). 20 pp.
Harry Mathews, *Out of Bounds* (poem sequence). 28 pp.
Friederike Mayröcker, *Heiligenanstalt*, trans. R. Waldrop. 96 pp.

Lissa McLaughlin, *Seeing the Multitudes Delayed* (stories).76 pp.
—, *Troubled by His Complexion* (stories).128 pp.
David Miller, *Stromata* (poems). 64 pp.
Claire Needell, *Not A Balancing Act* (poems). 64 pp.
Gale Nelson, *stare decisis* (poems). 142 pp.
—, *ceteris paribus* (poems). 128 pp.
Oskar Pastior, *Many Glove Compartments* (selected poems), trans.
    H. Mathews, C. Middleton, R. Waldrop, 120 pp.
Pascal Quignard, *Sarx*, trans. Keith Waldrop (poem). 40 pp.
—, *On Wooden Tablets: Apronenia Avitia* (novel), trans. Bruce X. 112 pp.
 Ray Ragosta, *Varieties of Religious Experience* (poems). 80 pp.
Ilma Rakusa, *Steppe*, trans. Solveig Emerson-Möring(stories). 80 pp.
Pam Rehm, *The Garment In Which No One Had Slept* (poems). 64 pp.
Jacqueline Risset, *The Translation Begins,* trans. Jennifer Moxley.96 pp.
Stephen Rodefer, *Passing Duration* (prose poems). 64 pp.
Claude Royet-Journoud, *i.e.* (poem), trans. Keith Waldrop. 20 pp.
Gerhard Rühm, *i my feet: selected poems & constellations.* 120 pp.
Brian Schorn, *Strabismus* (poems). 64 pp.
Esther Tellermann, *Mental Ground* (poem), trans. K. Waldrop. 80 pp.
Jane Unrue, *The House* (novella). 64 pp.
Alain Veinstein, *Even a Child, t*rans. R. Kocik and R. Waldrop. 64 pp.
Keith Waldrop, *The Space of Half an Hour* (3 poems). 88 pp.
Keith & Rosmarie Waldrop, *Ceci n'est pas Keith—Ceci n'est pas
    Rosmarie* (autobiographies). 94 pp.
Craig Watson, *After Calculus* (4 poems). 72 pp.
Marjorie Welish, *The Windows Flew Open* (poems). 80 pp.
Dallas Wiebe, *Going to the Mountain* (stories). 192 pp.
—, *Skyblue's Essays* (fictions). 160 pp.
—, *The Vox Populi Street Stories* (fiction). 312 pp.
Elizabeth Willis, *Turneresque* (poems). 96 pp.
Xue Di, *Heart Into Soil,* trans. Keith Waldrop with Wang Ping, Iona
    Crook, Janet Tan and Hil Anderson (poems). 96pp.

ANTHOLOGIES:
Norma Cole, ed./trans.,*Crosscut Universe: Writing on Writing from France.*160 pp.
One Score More: The Second 20 Years of Burning Deck 1982-2002. Edited
        by Alison Bundy, K. & R. Waldrop. 240 pp.
Pegasus Descending: A Book of the Best Bad Verse (anthology). Edited by James
        Camp, X.J.Kennedy, and Keith Waldrop. 238 pp.

I was a bastard to you, and I—"

She put her finger to his lips. "Enough. It's all in the past, and that's where I am going to leave it. Guess what? You should too."

Damon De Luca was a monster, a complete and total bastard. To his enemies, he was the nightmare no one wanted in their life.

To Milah De Luca, he was the love of her life, the man who saved her. He allowed her and only her to see him vulnerable. His greatest weakness was her, and he was hers. No one would ever find out.

This was how she would defeat the feud.

By loving this man so fiercely because she did love him with her whole heart, just as he loved her.

****

Damon stared down at his sleeping children.

Two babies, and another on the way.

He had never felt fear in his life. That day, five years ago, at the thought of losing Milah, he'd felt real fear.

She had never mocked him for it. Never held it against him, but Milah knew the key to his destruction.

He'd tried to stay in perfect control. To make Milah think she was just an object to some greater plan, but it was all a lie.

Damon fell in love with the fiery woman he'd seen on her birthday. That love had grown, and he'd watched her flourish into this very passionate woman he wanted by his side.

Turning off the bedroom light, he stepped out and moved toward his room. Milah sat on the bed, waiting for him.

His love.

His woman.

His reason to fucking breathe.

If anyone tried to take her from him, they would beg for death long before he gave it. She was his soul mate. His love. His everything, and only she would see this devotion.

The End

www.samcrescent.com

SAM CRESCENT

EVERNIGHT PUBLISHING ®

www.evernightpublishing.com

Made in United States
North Haven, CT
20 September 2022

24327661R00161